A Practical Guide to
Dragons

Inscribed by

Sindri Suncatcher

The Greatest Kender Wizard
Who Ever Lived

MIRRORSTONE

My dear Aunt Moonbeam,

You'll be proud to learn your nephew, the early
wanderer, has had quite a few fantastic adventures
over the past few years. I've battled an evil
sorceress raised from the dead, met not one,
but four amazing dragons, saved the world from
certain destruction at the hands of an undead
king, and made many new friends. Catriona
(that's one of my new friends) says
that I am all too eager to rush
into danger. But what's the
fun of learning new things
about the world if there isn't
a good bit of danger involved?

For now, though, mastering the art of
magic is my greatest goal. I've met a wizard
named Maddoc who has agreed to teach me everything
he knows. Just imagine, Aunt Moonbeam! It won't be
long before I can take the Test of High Sorcery and
fulfill my destiny as the greatest kender wizard who
ever lived, just as Mother predicted so many years ago.

I could fill a hundred scrolls with all the things
Maddoc has taught me so far. But since dragons
have only recently returned to our world, I thought
you and all the relatives would enjoy seeing this
book I've put together, chronicling what I've learned
from Maddoc about the great beasts. I'm positive it
won't be long before you catch sight of one of these
glorious creatures hovering over Kendermore.
As amazing as it will be, you should be
prepared for whatever may happen!

I will try to return home some
day soon. I cannot wait to
join you around the great stone
hearth in Cousin Phadri's hut
and tell the tales of my heroic
adventures. Till then, I hope
you'll treasure this book.

Sindri

Written overlooking the wooded hillside of Cairngorn Keep, Bleakcold, 355AC

ANATOMY OF A DRAGON

I once asked Maddoc whether a dragon was just an oversized lizard. He gave me a look that could match any ghoul's freezestare. "Lizards are a far inferior species, Apprentice," he said. "They do not live to be hundreds of years old, as a dragon does. They do not have wings, as a dragon does. But most of all, they do not have the sheer power and intelligence of dragonkind."

There are other differences too. Look at the dragon I drew here.

At first, I thought that dragon wings were like those of a bird. However, when I looked closer (which was not easy to do, let me tell you!), I realized a dragon's wings more closely resemble those of a bat. Bats, you see, have very long fingers, which form the frame of the wing. The tips of the fingers are actually visible. A dragon's wings are much the same.

The dragon uses its tail to help it steer as it flies. When swimming, the tail propels the dragon through the water. The dragon's tail is also the perfect weapon!

A dragon's body is covered with
hundreds of hard scales. They work
like a suit of armor, overlapping
each other to protect the body
beneath. The scales continue to
grow and multiply as the dragon
matures. They do not fall off, and
the dragon never sheds its skin.

A dragon's foot has three or four toes facing the front and one
facing sideways like a humanoid thumb. The toes are topped by
very sharp claws. A dragon can grasp objects, including wands
and weapons, with its feet.

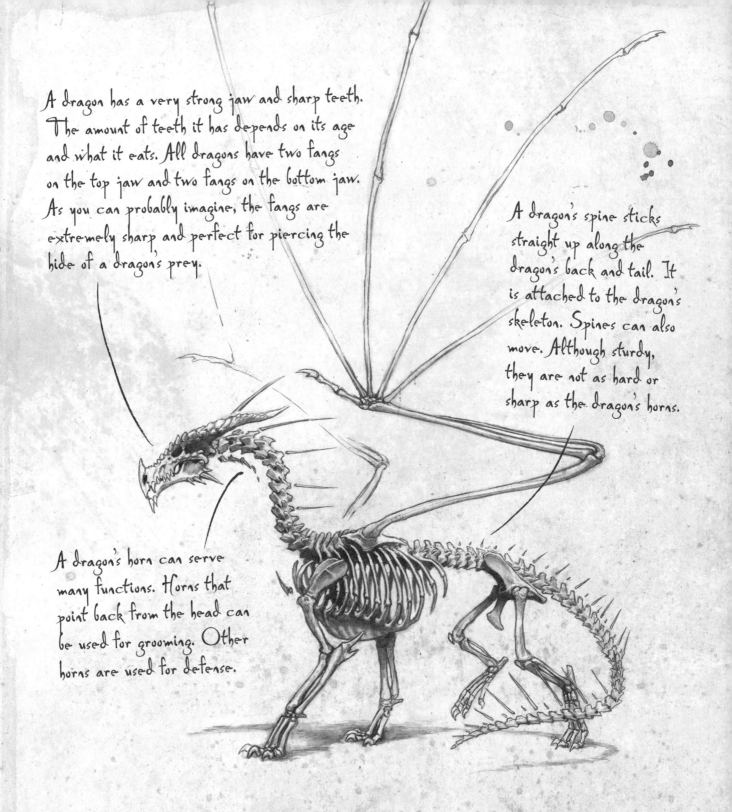

A dragon has a very strong jaw and sharp teeth. The amount of teeth it has depends on its age and what it eats. All dragons have two fangs on the top jaw and two fangs on the bottom jaw. As you can probably imagine, the fangs are extremely sharp and perfect for piercing the hide of a dragon's prey.

A dragon's spine sticks straight up along the dragon's back and tail. It is attached to the dragon's skeleton. Spines can also move. Although sturdy, they are not as hard or sharp as the dragon's horns.

A dragon's horn can serve many functions. Horns that point back from the head can be used for grooming. Other horns are used for defense.

A Look Inside a Dragon

Dragons have more than five hundred bones. I've counted! Sixty-eight bones alone make up the dragon's spine. I made this sketch the day Maddoc locked me in his ossuary. I don't know why he was so angry. All I did was conjure up the draconian egg he thought he had lost. I thought it was quite impressive.

Organs

Everyone knows dragons have huge brains, since they're so smart. But the most fascinating organ in a dragon's body is the draconis fundamentum. All of a dragon's blood passes through this organ before going through the rest of the body. Chemicals made in this organ move into the lungs, where the dragon's breath weapon is generated.

More about that later!

Dragon Senses

Sight: Exceptional
Adapted for hunting. Can judge distances with accuracy. Can see in dark.

Scent: Exceptional
Can sense others by scent.
Forked tongue helps in sniffing as well.

Hearing: Average
Similar to humans.

Taste: Exceptional
Dragons hate sweet flavors.

Why? Must ask next dragon I meet!

Touch: Poor
Cannot feel much thanks to thick skin and clawed feet.

Blindsense: Amazing!
Can see things that are invisible!
Can see even with their eyes closed.

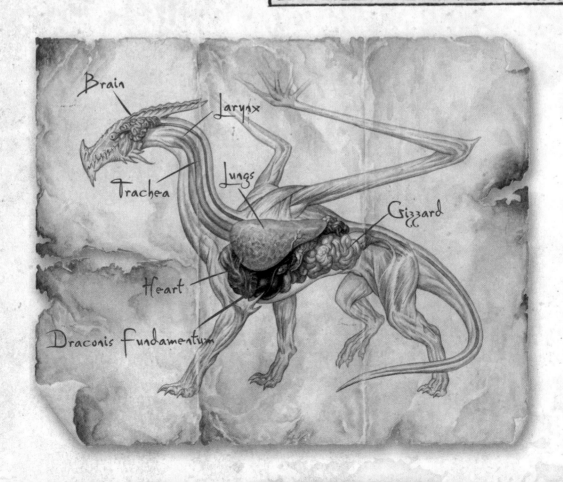

Brain

Larynx

Lungs

Gizzard

Trachea

Heart

Draconis Fundamentum

Muscles

Maddoc says an intact dragon corpse is even rarer than a dragon skeleton, but I have been lucky enough to see more than my fair share. According to Maddoc, a dragon's muscle system is similar to a cat's. The most amazing muscles of all are those that help the dragon fly. Because a dragon's bones are so light, and its muscles so strong, it is able to soar through the sky with relative ease.

Alar carpi ulnaris: allows wings to warp and twist

Alar deltoid: draws wing up and forward

Alar cleidomastoid: draws wing up and forward

Alar pectoral: main flight muscle

Walking

Running

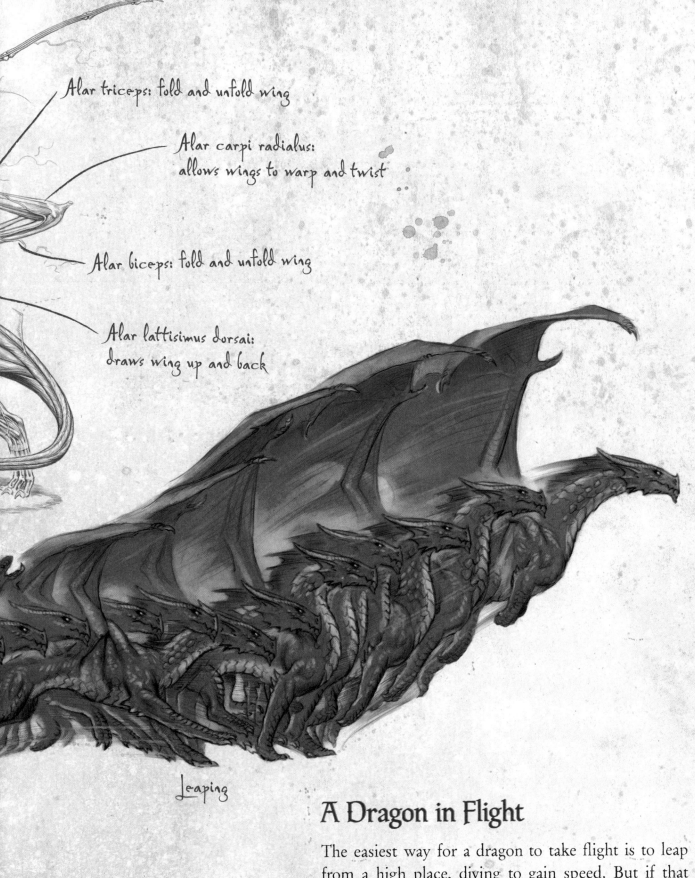

Alar triceps: fold and unfold wing

Alar carpi radialus:
allows wings to warp and twist

Alar biceps: fold and unfold wing

Alar lattisimus dorsai:
draws wing up and back

Leaping

A Dragon in Flight

The easiest way for a dragon to take flight is to leap from a high place, diving to gain speed. But if that isn't possible, it will leap into the air, snapping its tail downward and pushing off with its hind legs. Once aloft, a dragon can soar for hours with little effort.

DRAGON COMBAT

Dragons have a range of incredible natural weapons that they can use at any time to incapacitate their enemies.

Maddoc says, "A dragon is built for combat."

Breath Weapon

The most exciting is the dragon's breath weapon. The type of weapon is different from dragon to dragon, ranging from the chlorine gas of a green dragon to the slow gas from a copper. To use this weapon, a dragon takes a deep breath. If a dragon has enough chemicals in its lungs, then it can immediately blow out the breath weapon onto its victims.

Dragonfear

I've only heard tell of this natural weapon. But my friend Nearra told me dragonfear turns your muscles to ice, sends your heart racing, and makes your stomach feel as if it's clutched by a vice. I wish I could feel it myself. It sounds fascinating!

Magic

Maddoc says that dragons are born with a natural talent for spellcasting. (Kind of like me!) The spells they cast depend on their own unique personality. No scholar knows exactly how they come by this magical ability, but one day I intend to find out.

DRAGON FOOD

Dragons aren't picky eaters. They mostly like to eat meat—including kender, humans, dwarves, and elves! But anything (including rocks or dirt) will do. They can easily eat more than half their own weight in meat every day. Best of all, they never worry about getting fat.

Unlike poor uncle Oscar, may he rest in peace

TREASURE

Dragons love to hoard treasure. Some believe their love of treasure is similar to a kender's instinct to hoard bright, shiny objects. At any moment, a dragon will know the exact contents of its treasure pile and exactly how much it's worth.

DRAGON SOCIETY

Dragons are usually very solitary creatures. I don't know how they stand it. I like being in the midst of friends. Dragons, however, prefer their own company, and they often live alone in their lairs. The only exception might be when they are mating or perhaps raising wyrmlings. Although it has happened, it is very rare for dragons to unite and fight together against a foe. That is why you will usually encounter only one dragon at a time. Dragons sometimes fight one another, most often over treasure, lairs, or mates.

LANGUAGE OF DRAGONS

Maddoc's most interesting spellbooks are written in Draconic, the language of dragons. He says it is the oldest language around and that if I want to become like the most powerful wizards on Krynn, I must learn to speak it fluently. I'm supposed to memorize these words by tomorrow.

Common	Draconic	Common	Draconic
air	thrae	good	bensvelk
animal	baeshra	hate	dartak
armor	litrix	home	okarthel
arrow	svent	magic	arcaniss
ash	vignar	meat	rhyaex
axe	garurt	name	ominak
battle	vargach	night	thurkear
beautiful	vorel	no	thrice
big	turalisj	peace	martivir
bow	vaex	scroll	sjir
burn	valignat	secret	irthos
bravery	sveargith	see	ocuir
cave	waere	skin	molik
century	ierikc	song	miirik
claw	gix	speak	renthisj
dance	vaeri	stone	ternesj
danger	korth	strong	versvesh
day	kear	stupid	pothoc
dead	loex	sword	caex
dragon	darastrix	take	clax
earth	edar	talk	ukris
enchanted	levex	thief	virlym
fire	ixen	travel	ossalur
fly	austrat	treasure	rasvim
food	achthend	ugly	nurh
friend	thurirl	victory	vivex
gem	kethend	weapon	laraek
go	gethrisj	wizard	levethix

LIFE OF A DRAGON

Dragons begin life inside eggs. Where the eggs are laid depends on the kind of dragon. For example, the egg of a black dragon must be kept in strong acid. The egg of a white dragon must be buried in the snow. The color of the eggs match the color of the dragon who laid them. A mother dragon will lay a clutch of two to five eggs in a nest in her lair.

A young dragon is called a wyrmling. The wyrmling hatches from the egg, fully formed. At first they appear tiny and helpless. Their bodies are wet from the liquid inside the egg. After an hour, the wyrmlings dry off and they are able to fly. Wyrmlings inherit a vast amount of knowledge from their parents. Flying, hunting, reasoning—it is all instinctive and hereditary.

The Developmental Stages of the Dragon

Age	Dragon
0–5 years	Wyrmling
6–15 years	Very Young
16–25 years	Young
26–50 years	Juvenile
51–100 years	Young Adult
101–200 years	Adult
201–400 years	Mature Adult
401–600 years	Old
601–800 years	Very Old
801–1,000 years	Ancient
1,001–1,200 years	Wyrm
1,200+ years	Great Wyrm

A newly hatched wyrmling is small—no larger than a cat. Its instincts are to hunt for food and find a lair where it can live. For the next five years, the wyrmling will grow and learn. A dragon becomes a fully mature adult after about a hundred years. Maddoc gave me the chart here to show the age range of various stages of a dragon's life.

Dragons can live for more than a thousand years. Even an old dragon is still very active, and sometimes even more dangerous. Only when it reaches the great wyrm stage of its life do its body and mind finally stop developing. The dragon at this age is at the peak of its physical, mental, and magical abilities.

Brass Dragon

Blue Dragon

Red Dragon

Gold Dragon

White Dragon

Green Dragon

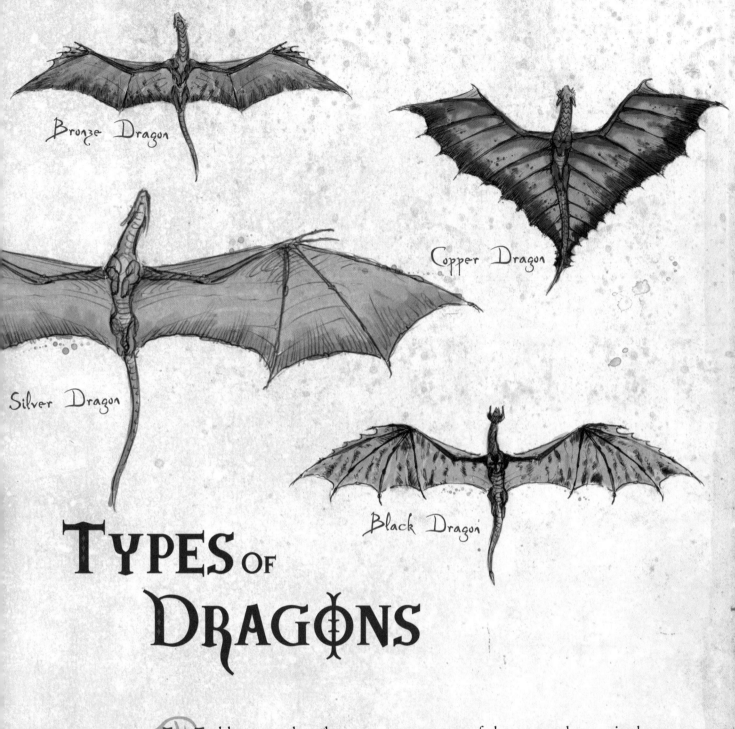

Bronze Dragon

Copper Dragon

Silver Dragon

Black Dragon

TYPES OF DRAGONS

Maddoc says that there are two groups of dragons—chromatic dragons and metallic dragons.

Chromatic dragons are black, blue, green, red, and white. These are the fierce, evil dragons. Catriona says it's best to avoid them. (But if you ask me, she's just upset because of the time that green dragon almost killed her. I find chromatics fascinating myself!)

Metallic dragons are brass, bronze, copper, gold, and silver. These dragons might not be as naturally evil as the chromatic dragons, but they must be respected. Metallic dragons do not choose to fight, but they will if provoked.

THE BLACK DRAGON

Black dragons are the most foul-tempered dragons. They are evil, mean, and extremely cunning. Some people call them skull dragons, and I'm sure you can see why. On an adult black dragon, it looks as if the scales are slowly wearing away, about to fall off in one foul batch.

The black dragon's major weapon is its breath. It shoots out a line of acid, sure to burn through most shields and wither most swords. The only black dragon I ever saw was a bit on the undead side, but I found it fascinating to look at all the same.

BLACK DRAGON FACTS

Maximum Height	16 feet
Maximum Weight	160,000 pounds
Maximum Wingspan	40 feet
Breath Weapon	Acid
Favorite Foods	Fish, mollusks, other aquatic creatures; some red meat from ground-dwelling animals
Habitat	Boggy swamps
Enemy	No natural enemy but will attack and kill almost anything
Favorite Treasure	Coins

The stinkier, the better!

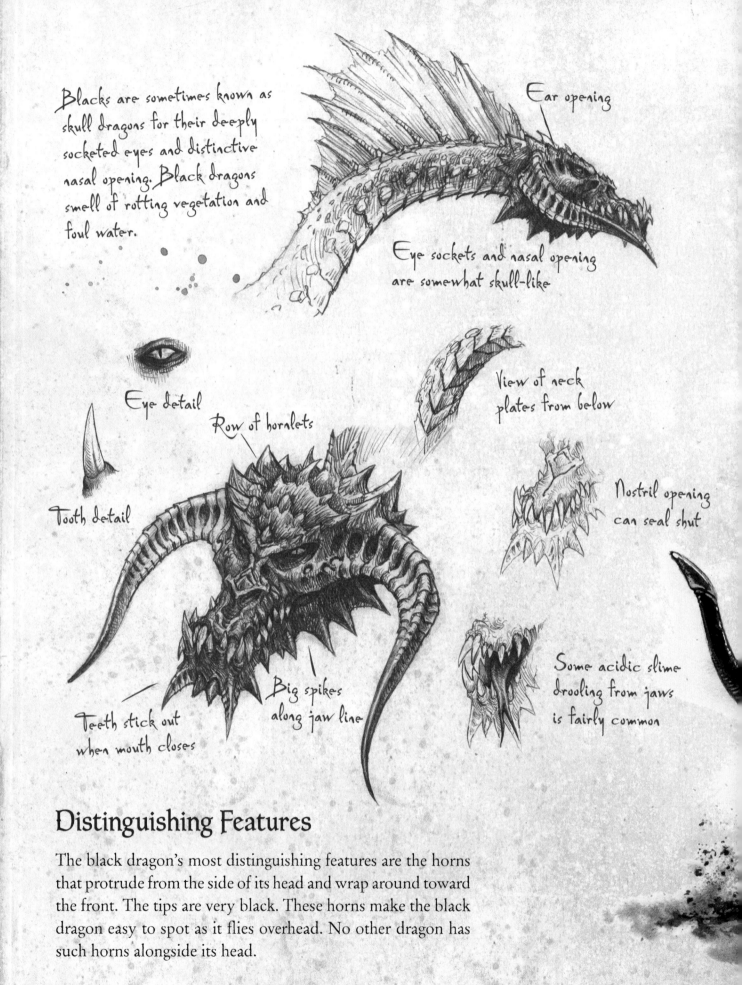

Blacks are sometimes known as skull dragons for their deeply socketed eyes and distinctive nasal opening. Black dragons smell of rotting vegetation and foul water.

Ear opening

Eye sockets and nasal opening are somewhat skull-like

Eye detail

Tooth detail

Row of hornlets

View of neck plates from below

Nostril opening can seal shut

Teeth stick out when mouth closes

Big spikes along jaw line

Some acidic slime drooling from jaws is fairly common

Distinguishing Features

The black dragon's most distinguishing features are the horns that protrude from the side of its head and wrap around toward the front. The tips are very black. These horns make the black dragon easy to spot as it flies overhead. No other dragon has such horns alongside its head.

Eggs

Female black dragons lay their eggs in swamps, marshes, or other boggy places, making the eggs nearly impossible to find. Besides being hard to find in such muddy places, the eggs must be submerged in strong acid.

Wyrmlings

Black dragons are cruel from the moment they are born. A wyrmling is extremely fierce and always hungry. The wyrmling has no conscience, and any creature can fall prey to the dragon's whims, including birds, small animals, and even plants.

Adults

As the black dragon matures, it becomes ever more devious. The black dragon frequently boasts about how superior it is, and it particularly enjoys taking things from others, not because it needs them, but because it can. As black dragons get older, they tend to spend more and more time in their lairs, surrounded by the coins they've collected over the years. It is unlikely that you would see a black dragon simply roaming about the countryside. They stick close to their lairs, hunting and swimming in the dark waters of the pond or swamp.

The Black Dragon's Lair

Black dragons live in caves or in underground chambers with numerous tunnels. Their lairs are usually next to a swamp or murky pond. Here, the black dragon will have an underwater entrance to its lair. The dragon's lair also has an above-ground entrance. You never know from which direction the black dragon may appear.

The black dragon's lair is often hard to spot because the dragon will usually cover the opening with plant growth. However, a quick sniff of the air will alert you that the lair is nearby. Their lairs often reek of the red meat the black dragons eat, for they like to let the meat sit in the pond until the meat has sufficiently pickled.

Combat

Black dragons are sneaky foes. They prefer to hide, then ambush their victims. Because they usually live in boggy, swampy areas, surrounded by trees, they will often hide among the plants or perhaps even within the swamp itself. The trees, however, prevent the black dragon from being able to fly upward too swiftly. This might be the only advantage you have if you must bring down a black dragon.

Typical Black Dragon Lair

Size of lair varies with size of dragon

Front View

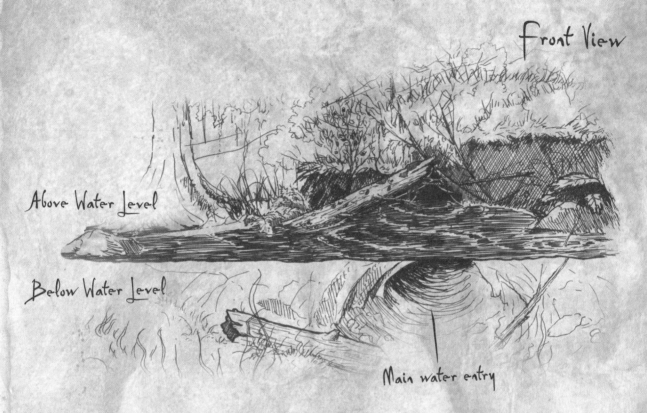

Above Water Level

Below Water Level

Main water entry

Profile View

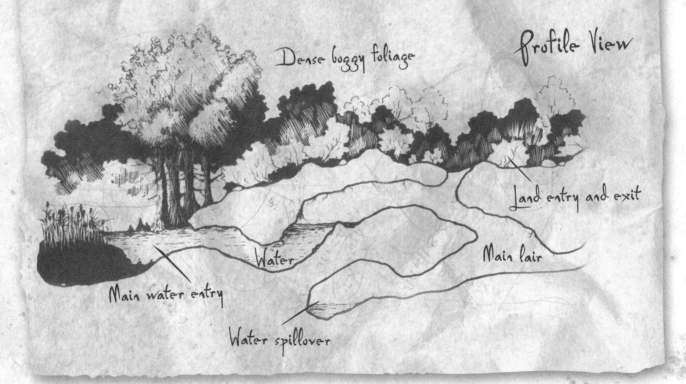

Dense boggy foliage

Land entry and exit

Main lair

Water

Main water entry

Water spillover

THE BLUE DRAGON

Blue dragons are much more talkative and outgoing than black dragons, but they still serve the cause of Darkness just as willingly. Blues tend to live in the desert. Maddoc says that they stick out like a sparkling sapphire in gritty pebbles of sand. Blues are especially well suited to aerial combat, with or without a rider. In battle, blue dragons do not issue fire or some other noxious vapor, as other dragons do. No, instead, from its mouth, the blue dragon shoots forth a bolt of lightning!

BLUE DRAGON FACTS

Maximum Height	16 feet
Maximum Weight	160,000 pounds
Maximum Wingspan	80 feet
Breath Weapon	Lightning
Favorite Foods	Meat from bigger animals, like camels; will also dine on snakes and lizards; if extremely hungry, and meat is scarce, will resort to eating plants
Habitat	Desert
Enemy	Brass dragons
Favorite Treasure	Sapphires

The blue dragon uses its lightning breath to cook its meals.

Blue dragons can't stand these dragons, mostly because they consider the brass dragon to be silly and carefree. I don't see what's so wrong with that myself.

Distinguishing Features

A blue dragon has one very distinctive horn on the top of its head, and the horn actually has two sharp points. One point is at the top of the horn, and the other is slightly below it. Another distinguishing feature is the blue dragon's ears, which are frilled like a blue morning glory flower. A blue dragon also has a thick, bumpy tail, like that of a caterpillar, and its wings are more pronounced and more batlike, with a claw protruding from the top of each.

Electrical attack

Build-up (hums and arcs)

Discharge (huge thunderclap)

Large, frilled external ear

Nostrils close to eye socket

Most teeth protrude when mouth is closed

Large triangular neck scales

Eyes/nostrils seal shut

Ears furl shut and dorsal spines flatten when burrowing

The hide of a blue dragon tends to crackle and hum faintly with built-up static electricity. These effects intensify when the dragon is angry or about to attack. They smell like electricity or sand.

Eggs

Despite all their evilness toward others, blue dragons are actually very good parents. They rarely leave a nest of eggs, which they bury in the sand. Once the eggs hatch, the blue dragon parents protect the wyrmlings, ensuring that the blue dragon society will continue to thrive.

Wyrmlings

A young blue dragon is adorable! Big, soft eyes and a softly rounded head. Even though it is no bigger than a large bird, like a hawk or an eagle, it can be extremely aggressive. It taunts and teases others into giving up their treasures, and it hunts small creatures to fill its belly.

Adults

Blue dragons like everything well ordered and that includes their own dragon society. An older, mature blue dragon usually presides over the younger blue dragons. It is very rare for one blue dragon to challenge another for this position. Blue dragons know their place, and if they are unhappy, they will simply leave and find their own territories.

As with all dragons, older blue dragons are quite clever, and they have an additional skill in their arsenal of tricks: hallucination. An older blue dragon can make the land appear to be something it is not, such as a fresh lake of water. However, the older a blue dragon becomes, the more loud and obnoxious is its character. It may have many tricks to fool you, but you will also hear it laughing a sound that makes most creatures freeze in their tracks.

Typical Blue Dragon Lair

Size of lair varies with size of dragon

Profile View

Ledge exit

Upper chamber

Main entry (hidden)

Pool (lower chamber)

Mid chamber

Sandy beach

Plan View

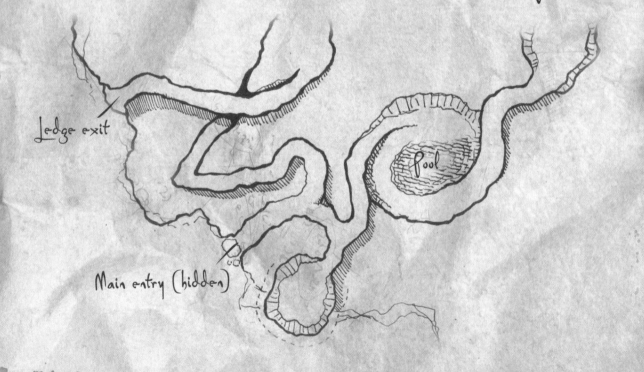

Ledge exit

Pool

Main entry (hidden)

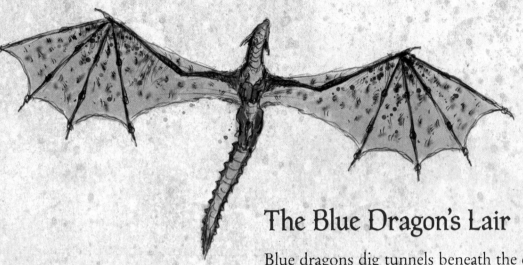

The Blue Dragon's Lair

Blue dragons dig tunnels beneath the desert ground and high up into towering rock formations. Such a construction gives the blue dragon several advantages. The blue dragon can slink out of its cave along the ground, the opening of which is hidden by sand, or it can perch high up on a ledge and survey its territory.

Inside, the blue dragon's lair has many tunnels and several chambers. An upper chamber can be found within the rocky mountain, and a middle chamber can be found beneath the desert ground. A tunnel winds even farther downward, and here you will find a lower chamber, where the blue dragon has found the water that runs below ground. The water forms a pool, in which the blue dragon will wallow and rest and drink.

Combat

An attack from a blue dragon can come from above—or from below! A blue dragon will burrow beneath the sand and wait there for its next victim. Its horns might protrude from the desert sand, but some often mistake the horn for a spiky desert rock. Seeking some shade cast by this supposed "rock," an adventurer will rest beside it only to have the ground rumble and come alive. So if you want to find a blue dragon, watch out for any pointy rocky protrusions you might see in the desert— they might not be a rocks at all!

THE GREEN DRAGON

My friends and I had the honor of actually battling a young green dragon named Slean. She was my very first dragon encounter, and I must admit, I was so excited when she circled above us. I could hardly wait for her to fly down to us, but my friends kept me quiet and prevented me from calling out to her. Even though I felt the fear in them, I still did not quite understand just how evil a green dragon could be. All I wanted was to get closer to her, to see her up close. It wasn't long before Slean spotted us and was soon upon us. But that's another story. . . .

GREEN DRAGON FACTS

Maximum Height	10 feet
Maximum Weight	160,000 pounds
Maximum Wingspan	80 feet
Breath Weapon	Chlorine gas
Favorite Foods	Little folk such as gnomes *and kender!*
Habitat	Forests with tall trees
Enemy	Green dragons sometimes clash with black dragons over the choicest lairs
Favorite Treasure	Mementos of particularly exciting victories

Distinguishing Features

From the air, a green dragon looks like a giant green snake with wings. Its neck and tail are thickest toward the wings; then they taper off into a soft, rounded point. The green dragon's neck is long and elegant, like that of a swan. As the green dragon gets nearer, you see one of its most amazing features: a large, waving crest that starts at the dragon's nose and runs the entire length of the dragon's body. If you were to look down or upward at the dragon, you might not see this crest. From the side, however, it is most extraordinary! I must say that although many of my friends that fateful day were overcome by dragonfear, I was enraptured by Slean's magnificent crest and graceful greenery.

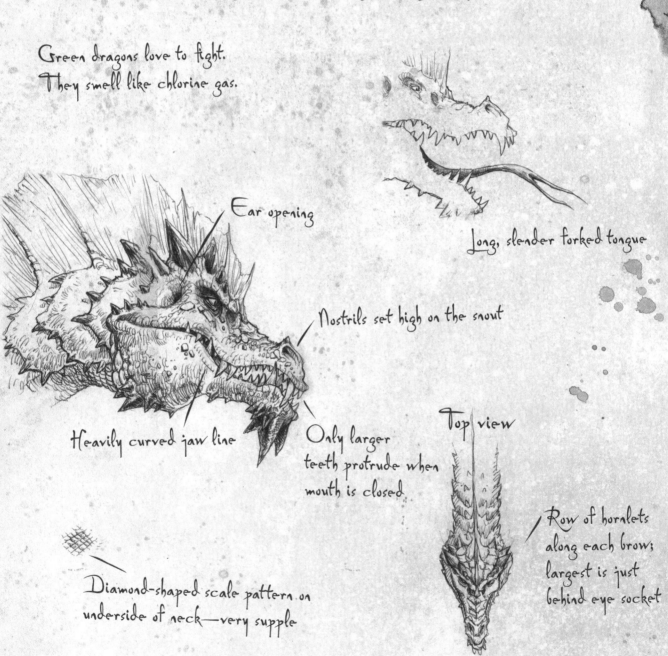

Green dragons love to fight.
They smell like chlorine gas.

Long, slender forked tongue

Ear opening

Nostrils set high on the snout

Heavily curved jaw line

Only larger teeth protrude when mouth is closed

Top view

Row of hornlets along each brow; largest is just behind eye socket

Diamond-shaped scale pattern on underside of neck—very supple

Eggs

A green dragon keeps her eggs in a solution of acid or buries them in leaves moistened with rainwater. Both parents will rarely leave their eggs while the eggs are incubating.

Wyrmlings

If you encounter a green dragon wyrmling, you might at first mistake it for the wyrmling of a black dragon. That is because the scales of a wyrmling green dragon are very dark, nearly black. As the wyrmling matures, the scales become lighter and brighter, until they become a magnificent green shade. Wyrmlings usually stay with both parents until they reach adulthood, which could be a hundred years. So if you see a young green, keep on alert—the mother and father might not be far behind.

Adults

Adult green dragons are extremely territorial, which means if you are fortunate enough to stumble into a forest inhabited by a green dragon, you have to be extra crafty. You might be able to bribe the green dragon into letting you walk through the forest, but remember that greens are good liars and sweet-talkers. The green dragon might pretend to agree to let you go, when all she is doing is merely playing with you. You have to be clever to outsmart an adult green dragon.

The Green Dragon's Lair

If you are ever looking for a green dragon, the best place to start is at a waterfall. Specifically, climb up the cliff over which the waterfall tumbles and look behind the cascading water. Can you find a cave hidden behind the falls? If you do, most likely, you have come upon the entrance of a green dragon's lair.

Green dragons would much prefer to live in a cave high up on a cliff. (The better to see all of their domain!) However, green dragons have been known to have lairs below ground, by which they enter through a pond or a lake. If you think it sounds a bit similar to the lair of a black dragon, you are right! Black dragons and green dragons might sometimes battle for the perfect lair. Once a green dragon has its sights set on a black dragon's lair, it will not willingly give it up. It might not fight for it, but it will wait until the black dragon dies, no matter how long that might take.

Combat

Green dragons love combat, and they will attack for no reason, especially if they find you in their territory. Greens thrive on power, and they love intrigue and double-crossing others. Green dragons might appear rude to their own kind, but to others, green dragons are smooth talkers.

Typical Green Dragon Lair

Size of lair varies with size of dragon

Oblique View

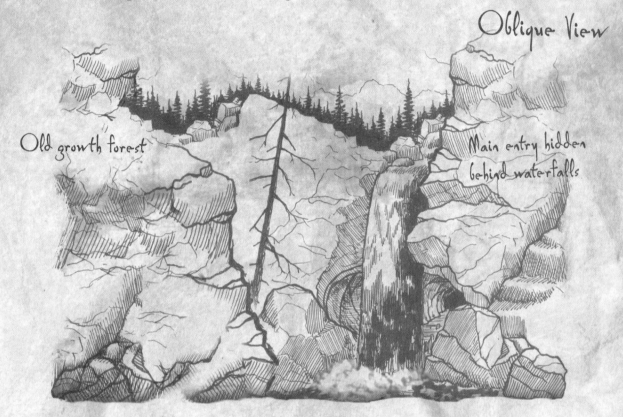

Old growth forest

Main entry hidden behind waterfalls

Plan View

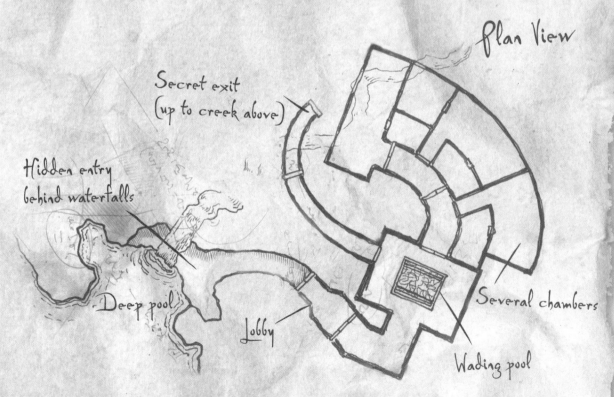

Secret exit (up to creek above)

Hidden entry behind waterfalls

Deep pool

Lobby

Several chambers

Wading pool

THE RED DRAGON

Of all the chromatic dragons, the red dragon is the most feared. Reds are ferocious and cruel, and they think nothing of inflicting pain wherever they may be.

One of my favorite stories is of a red dragon named Kiernan the Crimson. He would attack traveling caravans, demanding treasure in exchange for people's lives. Kiernan hunted very near the Temple of the Holy Orders of the Stars, a most sacred place. When a temple cleric, named Elethia heard of Kiernan, she ordered the dragon to leave. Red dragons are always willing to fight, and Kiernan was no different. But Elethia had the gods on her side. She shot an arrow, which pierced and Kiernan tumbled to the ground, dead. Most people who encounter a red dragon are not as lucky.

Red dragons claim they are the most tasty!

RED DRAGON FACTS

Maximum Height	22 feet
Maximum Weight	1,280,000 pounds
Maximum Wingspan	150 feet
Breath Weapon	Fire *Naturally!*
Favorite Foods	Humans, most particularly females; young elves
Habitat	Mountains or hilly plains
Enemy	Silver dragons
Favorite Treasure	Absolutely anything with some monetary value

When the two come in conflict, silver dragons almost always win!

An angry red may have flames licking up from eyes and nostrils. Their pupils fade as they age, until the oldest have eyes with the appearance of molten orbs. They smell like smoke and sulphur.

Horns vary greatly and can be bone-white to black, straight or twisted.

Brow horns

Lizard-like skull (not an alligator!)

Cheekbone horns   Jaw horns (May merge with ear frill on older dragons)

Small nose horn

Single, back-swept frill on neck

Chin horns

Forked tongue

Distinguishing Features

Red dragons, of course, are a stunning red color, quite hard to miss, actually. What's also hard to miss, if a dragon is gliding above you, are the red dragon's horns. They point back along the dragon's head toward its wings. Red dragons' wings are the largest and longest of any dragon, stretching more than the length of the entire beast. The fringe along the bottom of the wings is tinged a purplish blue.

Eggs

The eggs of a red dragon must be kept in an open flame at all times. After the eggs are laid, the younger of the two parents (whether male or female) will stay behind to guard the eggs and keep the nest of flames burning. Once hatched, the wyrmlings are left alone to fend for themselves.

Wyrmlings

Wyrmlings are really just smaller versions of their parents, in nearly all ways. They are selfish and greedy, and they have no problem destroying things. Although no larger than a cat, the wyrmling does not let its small size stop it from wreaking havoc on just about anything that moves—a trait that the wyrmling will take into adulthood.

Adults

Red dragons spend their adulthood collecting treasure and attacking foes when necessary. All dragons love to hoard, but the red dragon is the biggest hoarder of them all. They can recognize the value of any object, from the largest bauble to the tiniest trinket.

They slow down as they get older, although they never lose their evil nature. Instead of venturing from their lairs to do harm, they choose to stay well within their pits, enjoying the treasures they've collected over their lifetime.

The Red Dragon's Lair

The perfect home for a red dragon is . . . where else? In the smoldering, fiery depths of a volcano. If a volcano is not convenient, however, a red dragon will reside within any mountain, as long as it provides an excellent ledge on which the red dragon can perch to view its territory.

The entrance to the red dragon's lair is well above the ground, some hundred feet or more, so be sure to brush up on your climbing skills if you want to see a red's lair! An entrance chamber leads to a narrow tunnel, which drops off into a steep, dark pit. If you climb into the pit, you'll find a pool of water surrounded by several chambers. One chamber serves as the dragon's sleeping quarters. The other chamber contains the dragon's hoard.

Combat

Red dragons are confident fighters. They will spend years building battle strategies and patiently wait until the best moment to call upon them. They are fast in the air, but a bit clumsy, so they prefer to do their fighting on the ground.

Typical Red Dragon Lair

Size of lair varies with size of dragon

Plan View

Ledge Entrance

Pit

False Chamber

Pool

Storage Chamber

Sleeping Chamber

Entry View

Cut-Away View

Pit

150 ft. drop into cavern below

Pool

THE WHITE DRAGON

The white dragon is not quite as big as the other chromatics, nor is it as fierce. During the War of the Lance, the whites were called upon to guard the southern region of Icewall, and I hear that you can still find some whites with their dragon highlords living in those parts.

White dragons are beautiful creatures to behold, with stunning white scales and wings tinged a pinkish blue. Whites are most intent on looking for food. You can see it in their dark, piercing eyes. The eyes size up anything they come across, with the only purpose of deciding if that morsel is truly something good to eat. Then the white dragon engages its breath weapon, and zap!

Maddoc just told me this is called cryogenic attack!

WHITE DRAGON FACTS

Maximum Height	16 feet
Maximum Weight	160,000 pounds
Maximum Wingspan	72 feet
Breath Weapon	Frost
Favorite Foods	Anything that moves, but it must be frozen first!
Habitat	High mountains
Enemy	Red dragons
Favorite Treasure	Anything sparkly and shiny, especially diamonds!

But the whites usually stay far out of the reds' way!

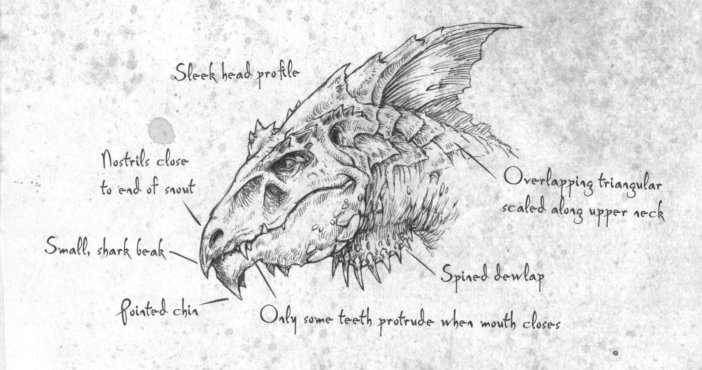

Sleek head profile

Nostrils close
to end of snout

Overlapping triangular
scaled along upper neck

Small, shark beak

Spined dewlap

Pointed chin

Only some teeth protrude when mouth closes

Cryogenic attack

Whites are the smallest and
least intelligent of dragonkind.
They have a crisp, faintly
chemical odor.

Distinguishing Features

The scales of the white dragon are, of course, a wonderful white color, and they seem to sparkle and glitter in the sun. But there are other features as well. Take a look at its head and neck. Don't they seem to blend into each other, with no distinguishing features at all? Don't the wings look a bit frayed along the edges? That's another sign of the white dragon.

Now look at the white dragon's chin. The white dragon has a flap of skin, and along this flap lies a row of spines. And notice the shape of the white dragon's head. It's rather streamlined, isn't it? From the tip of the dragon's sharp snout to the crests that stagger up the dragon's head, the head as a whole forms a nice, fluid line. This streamlined head helps the dragon soar through the sky.

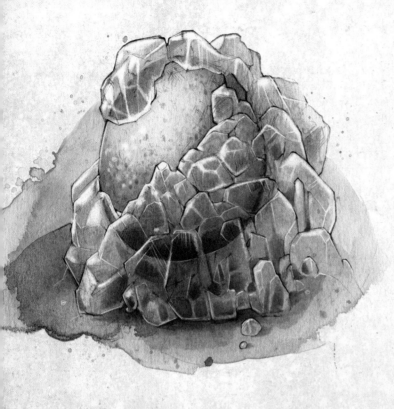

Eggs

White dragons tend to lay their eggs in the snow or encase them in ice. They don't bother with tending their eggs, but they will lay them near their lairs.

Wyrmlings

A newly born wyrmling has scales as clear as ice. The scales will become white as the wyrmling grows. Although wyrmlings are expected to survive on their own from the moment they are born, some white dragon parents will let the wyrmling live in their lair.

Adults

Mature white dragons have some amazing abilities. They can climb ice cliffs with their talons. They can soar through the sky like a freezing wind. They enjoy swimming in icy cold waters, and they will often prowl frozen seas and oceans for large animals to eat, even whales. White dragons often become more savage as they mature, always on the hunt for food.

Having lived their entire lives in the shadows of more powerful dragons, whites often develop a chip on their shoulders. Older whites tend to pick on bigger fellows, such as giants and other dragons. In this way, the white dragon feels it has gotten revenge for all the times in its past when it has been bested by bigger creatures.

Typical White Dragon Lair
Size of lair varies with size of dragon

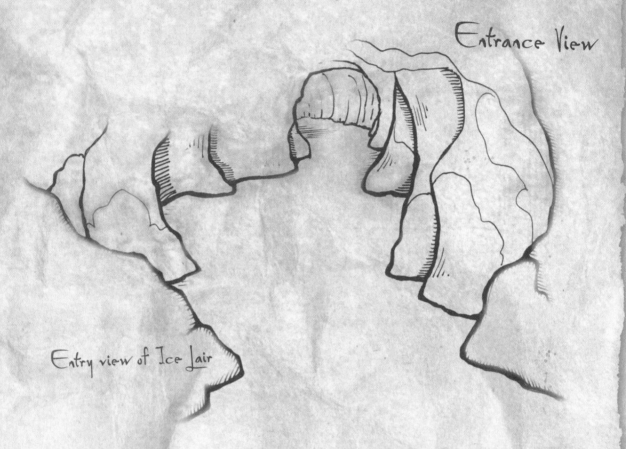

Entrance View

Entry view of Ice Lair

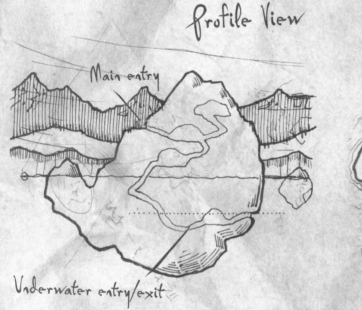

Profile View

Main entry

Underwater entry/exit

Plan View

Main entry

Underwater entry/exit

The White Dragon's Lair

White dragons live in ice caves, usually dug into the side of a mountain. The white dragon has a wonderful lair, full of tunnels carved out of ice. The tunnels lead to a multitude of chambers, where you might find the white dragon resting or perhaps even attending to a young wyrmling or two. A white dragon might also reside in an iceberg, floating atop a mountain lake or on a frigid ocean or sea. The white dragon will use the entire space of the berg, both above and below water.

Although they do not need a lofty perch for their lairs, they sometimes find themselves in competition with a red dragon. The white dragon knows that it is no match for the red dragon, and it usually slinks off to find its own nesting place. And because the red dragon knows that the white dragon is no threat, the red dragon usually lets the white dragon do its slinking.

Combat

White dragons aren't the smartest dragons, but they do have remarkable memories. A white dragon remembers most things that it experiences, which can be quite a curse if you ever cross a white dragon. The white dragon will never forget it, and it will hunt you mercilessly, seeking revenge.

THE BRASS DRAGON

Unlike the previous dragons I've covered, the brass dragon is a metallic and probably one of the most dazzling specimens of them all. Ah, how the metallics can dazzle even the most jaded of dragon hunters. And it's quite amazing, really, for the metallics do not enthrall us with their evil ways, as the chromatics do. (Or is it only me who is enthralled by the chromatics?) No, the metallic dragons enrapture us with their stunning scales, as well as their incredible goodness.

The brass dragon loves to talk, and it often ensnares unsuspecting travelers in a bout of long-winded conversation. The brass dragon might also be the most humble of all dragons.

Maddoc says the brass dragon is the most like me. Not sure what he means by that!

BRASS DRAGON FACTS

Maximum Height	16 feet
Maximum Weight	160,000 pounds
Maximum Wingspan	60 feet
Breath Weapon	Fire and sleep gas
Favorite Foods	Dew drops
Habitat	Desert
Enemy	Blue Dragons
Favorite Treasure	Objects made out of plant materials. Examples: A rare piece of wood, a finely woven garment, and so on.

A fact I find amazing: For such a large beast, the brass dragon actually consumes very little. Is it possible that the brass dragon is aware of the delicate balance of its desert home?

Perhaps because there are so few plants in the desert?

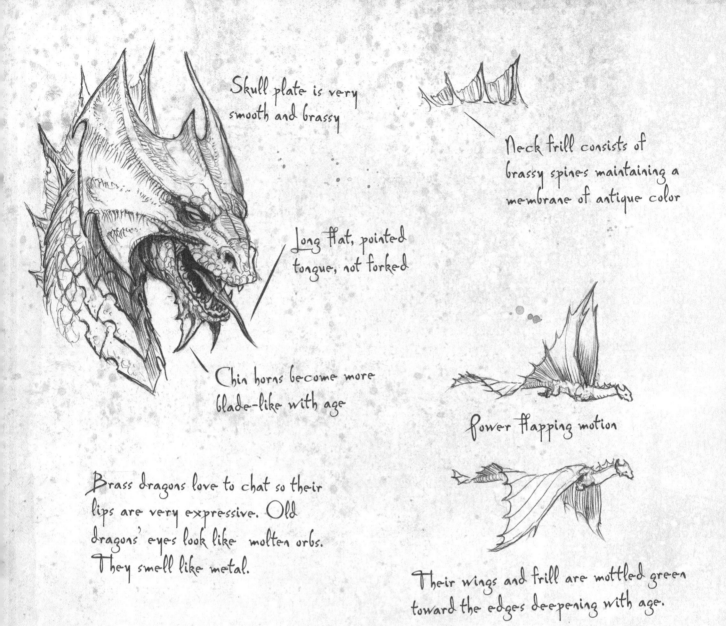

Skull plate is very smooth and brassy

Neck frill consists of brassy spines maintaining a membrane of antique color

Long flat, pointed tongue, not forked

Chin horns become more blade-like with age

Power flapping motion

Brass dragons love to chat so their lips are very expressive. Old dragons' eyes look like molten orbs. They smell like metal.

Their wings and frill are mottled green toward the edges deepening with age.

Distinguishing Features

When seen from below, the brass dragon is quite unmistakable. Its outstretched wings form a triangular shape. And, unlike most dragons, the brass dragon's wings are attached along its body all the way to the tip of its tail. The wings are longest at the shoulder, and they taper off quite wonderfully as they reach the tail.

If a brass dragon lands and starts to talk to you, you will become enamored by two features. Its brilliant brass scales will seem to radiate heat with their pleasant, brassy glow. The other feature you will notice right away is the shape of its head. The head is not round or oval, like that of most creatures. Instead, the head has a dramatic curved plate that extends from the dragon's eyes and cheeks, and it curves upward into two points. Quite stunning, really. The brass dragon also has two sharp horns on its chin, and these horns become more pointy as the brass dragon ages.

Eggs

Brass dragon eggs reside in a nest of open flame, similar to a red dragon's eggs. However, they will hatch after 480 days, unlike the red dragon's eggs, which will take 660 days to incubate.

Wyrmlings

A newly born brass dragon is not all that remarkable. Its scales are a dull, unimpressive brown. At first glance, you might mistake the wyrmling for no more than an glorified lizard, hiding in the sand. As it matures, though, the scales become the warm, burnished brass that is so striking, especially when struck by the rays of the hot desert sun. And like its elders, the wyrmling is born with the gift of gab. It will talk on and on and on, at times about seemingly nothing. It will talk to animals that can't talk back. It will even talk to itself if no one is near.

Adults

Along with its love of speech, the adult brass dragon loves fire. It finds the flames quite beautiful, and it can often stare at the fire for hours. So entranced might the young adult become that it doesn't realize what it might be burning!

Aging brass dragons sometimes feel that they have seen enough of the world. They feel that others are ruining the world, and the brass dragon has no problem stating its opinion for one and all to hear. Yet as it becomes ancient, the brass dragon seems to accept the folly of others, and it may often donate some of its treasures to help out a cause that it feels is worthy. Always ready to offer advice—and to hear itself talk—the brass dragon is definitely a dragon I would be happy to call my friend.

If I were ever fortunate to meet one!

The Brass Dragon's Lair

Like the blue dragon, the brass dragon prefers to dig its home in a desert peak or spire. The brass dragon also prefers that part of its lair face the rising desert sun, which will warm the rocks and keep the brass dragon quite toasty throughout the day. But unlike the blue dragon's home, which is really just one long tunnel, the brass dragon's lair is a series of tunnels that weaves in and out and all about. Some tunnels lead to dead ends. But the true tunnels lead—where else?—to the Grand Conversation Hall. It is really quite a sophisticated room for a dragon, with straight, high walls and steps leading from a foyer down into it.

The brass dragon's lair does not have a main entrance. Instead, the brass dragon digs several small entrances, called bolt holes. The holes are often covered by wind-blown sand, but the brass dragon always knows where they are. The dragon can dive into any one of these holes to escape a blue dragon, and the blue dragon will be none the wiser. (Although blue dragons are much more deadly, the brass dragon can usually outrun its long-time nemesis.)

Combat

Brass dragons would much rather talk than fight. But if you fail to engage in a brass dragon's conversation, the dragon just might blast you with its sleep gas! The brass dragon also uses its sleep gas to knock out any creature it finds threatening. But in the face of real danger, the brass dragon will most likely simply fly away and hide in the sand.

Typical Brass Dragon Lair

Size of lair varies with size of dragon

Oblique View

Plan View

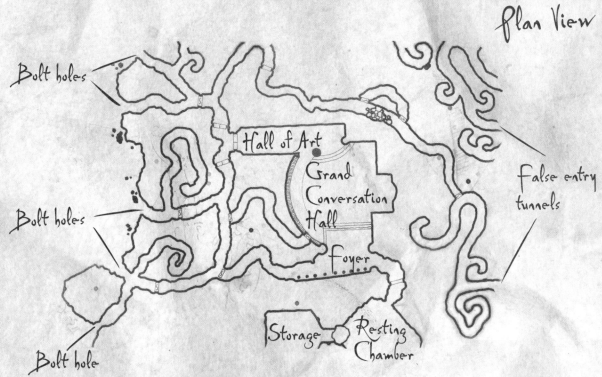

Bolt holes

Bolt holes

Bolt hole

Hall of Art

Grand Conversation Hall

Foyer

False entry tunnels

Storage

Resting Chamber

THE BRONZE DRAGON

Bronze dragons love to take on the form of smaller creatures—especially humans. For bronze dragons truly enjoy humans. In fact, bronze dragons enjoy humans so much that they often go out of their way to help them. They may save sea-goers stuck in a storm or rescue humans from a dangerous foe. In many instances, the bronze dragon transforms itself into a human, so those who are rescued never know who did the rescuing. Bronze dragons do not seek payment for their help. Their reward is simply to know that a life has been saved.

BRONZE DRAGON FACTS

Maximum Height	10 feet
Maximum Weight	160,000 pounds
Maximum Wingspan	80 feet
Breath Weapon	Cone of repulsion gas, line of lightning
Favorite Foods	Aquatic plants; some seafood (shark meat is a tantalizing treat, and bronze dragons may spend some time hunting sharks); pearls are another delicacy
Habitat	Near water, and warm, temperate climates preferred
Enemy	Evil sea creatures
Favorite Treasure	Pearls, coral, intricate shells, and gold

A tropical island, for example, is a perfect habitat for a bronze dragon.

Distinguishing Features

The color bronze is rather hard to describe, I find. It's not as orange as brass or copper, but more of a tarnished brown, if you will. The wings of a bronze dragon may be tipped with green, so that may help you identify it. What will really help, however, are the horns that sweep back from the dragon's head. The bronze dragon has three horns on each side of its cheeks; these horns bend back toward its tail, and more two horns perch at the top of its head. Each horn is capped by a very sharp, dark-colored point.

Small head frill

Great Wyrm

Purple grey tongue is long and pointed, not forked

Hatchling

Tall neck frill though not as tall as the silver

Powerful swimmers, bronze dragons have webbed feet and membranes behind their forelimbs. Their scales are smooth and flat. They smell like sea-spray. Great wyrms have glowing green orbs for eyes.

Chin horns

Old Bronze

Young Adult

Eggs

Bronze dragons mate for life, and they take parenting very seriously. They will protect their eggs and their offspring at all costs. Although these dragons love the sea, they always lay their eggs in a dry cave, never underwater.

Wyrmlings

Bronze dragon wyrmlings are quite lucky, actually. For unlike many dragons, the bronze wyrmling has the attention of both its parents. The wyrmling at first appears yellow, with a twinge of green around its scales. The yellow will slowly turn into a rich brown bronze as the wyrmling matures. Wyrmlings frolic in the ocean like dolphins, although they can prove a bit troublesome to people who fish the waters.

Adults

Bronze dragons always seek justice, and they cannot stand to see other creatures being treated with cruelty. If anything, this quality becomes even more pronounced with age. Bronze dragons are perhaps the most social of all the dragons. They love to romp with other bronzes, often swimming and playing together. If you have a festival scheduled, a group of bronzes might congregate and attend, although you wouldn't know it! They will assume a different form so they can observe and participate in your party.

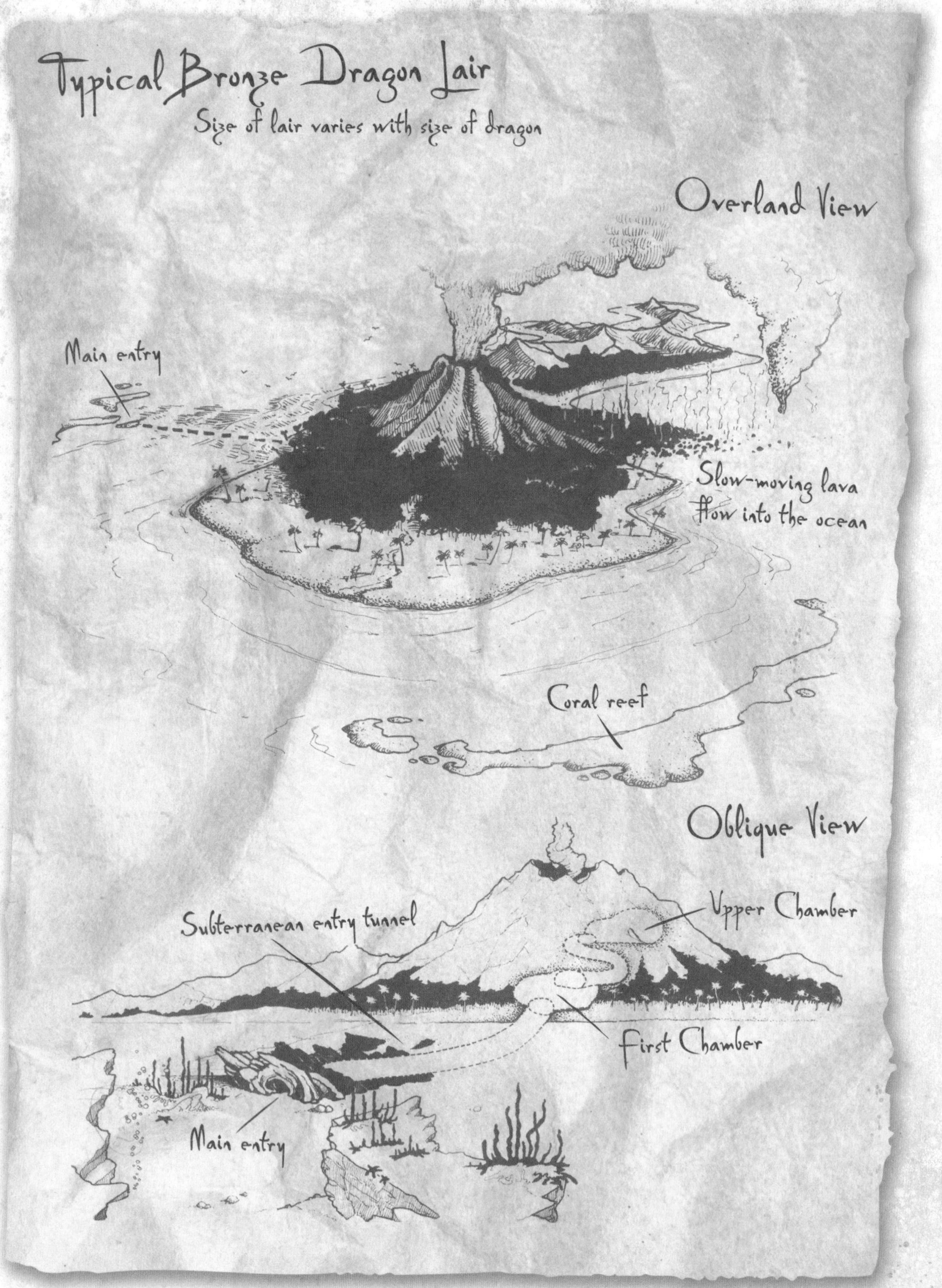

Typical Bronze Dragon Lair

Size of lair varies with size of dragon

Overland View

Main entry

Slow-moving lava flow into the ocean

Coral reef

Oblique View

Subterranean entry tunnel

Upper Chamber

First Chamber

Main entry

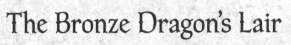

The Bronze Dragon's Lair

Unless you have the ability to swim and breathe underwater, you probably won't find the entrance to the bronze dragon's lair. Because the bronze is a highly adept swimmer, the opening to its lair is totally submerged beneath the water. The entrance may be obscured by the wavy fronds of seaweed or disguised as multi-armed coral. Upon entering the cavelike opening, you will find yourself in a long tunnel. The tunnel will gradually slant upward, until you reach dry land. Keep going, and eventually you will come to the first chamber of the dragon's lair, which is usually dug level with the land. If your bronze dragon happened to have dug its lair inside a volcano (the home of choice!), then another tunnel will lead you farther upward. Eventually the tunnel will end at another chamber, perhaps one thousand feet above the ground.

Combat

Bronze dragons find battles quite fascinating, and they may join armies to help good defeat evil. In battle they have several breath weapons at their disposal. One is a cone of repulsion gas. The gas is so stinky that creatures within its cone are totally repulsed. Their only thought once the foul air has been exhaled is to get as far away from the dragon as possible. It's quite effective! Bronze dragons have also been known to emit a line of lightning, although they will only do so if they are protecting others. Bronze dragons may also create a fog cloud (an intriguing spell-like ability), which completely blinds its foes. Once an enemy has lost its sight, the bronze dragon will pick it up and carry it far away, to a place where it can do no harm, such as a deserted island, perhaps. In this way, the bronze dragon keeps others safe while sticking to its strong standard of not killing unless absolutely necessary.

THE COPPER DRAGON

The copper dragon loves to play tricks, and it is a natural-born jokester. It may disguise itself as a rock, then spring into action to surprise unwary travelers. Because the copper dragon is metallic, it is not evil and it means no harm—even though its tricks can seem quite devious. They simply love to impress us with their sharp wit and fool us with their clever pranks.

And I should know, for I actually met a copper dragon! More about that later.

COPPER DRAGON FACTS

Maximum Height	16 feet
Maximum Weight	160,000 pounds
Maximum Wingspan	80 feet
Breath Weapon	Slow gas and line of acid
Favorite Foods	Enormous scorpions and other venomous creatures
Habitat	Dry, rocky mountains
Enemy	Red and blue dragons
Favorite Treasure	Valuables from the earth: metals and precious stones, as well as finely sculpted statues and well-crafted ceramics

I've never had a chance to taste one myself, but the copper dragons claim that the venom makes their wit that much sharper!

Distinguishing Features

The color of a copper dragon may be hard to distinguish from that of a brass dragon, but the copper dragon is a bit deeper in hue. Also the copper dragon has a hint of blue along the edge of its scales and wings.

From above, the copper dragon also slightly resembles a brass dragon, for its wings also form a triangular shape. The copper dragon, however, has elbows that make a pronounced dip. This dip gives the wings more of a V shape than a triangular shape.

Coppers are powerful jumpers and climbers with massive thighs and shoulders. As they age, their pupils fade to glowing turquoise. They have a stony odor.

Broad flat horns appear plated

Ear hole

Long, pointed tongue, not forked

Adult

Great Wyrm

Teeth don't show when mouth is closed

Two long, flat, smooth coppery horns

Old Copper

Jaw frill

Twin ridges of overlapping plates on back of neck

Hatchling

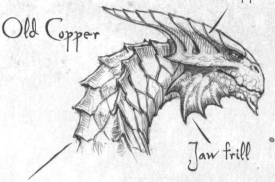

Eggs

Coppers lay their eggs in a nest of cool sand or clay.

Wyrmlings

The scales of a copper wyrmling are a muddy brown color, and they will slowly turn a beautiful glowing copper as the wyrmling matures. Both parents raise the wyrmling until it reaches adulthood; then the parents part ways.

Adults

Adults are quite social because, naturally, they need someone else around in order to play their tricks.

I'll never forget the day I met Raedon, a wonderful friend and a copper dragon! This is from my journal, the day we met.

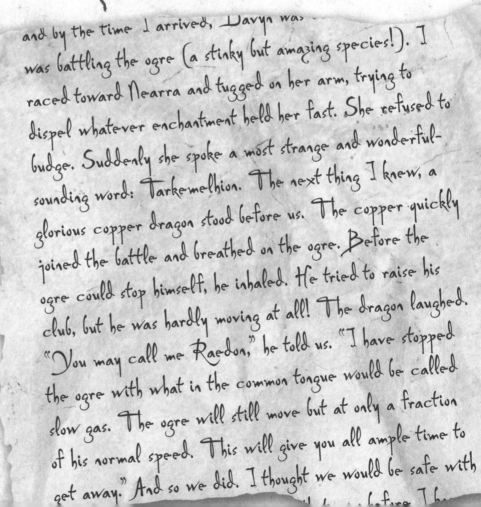

and by the time I arrived, Davyn was was battling the ogre (a stinky but amazing species!). I raced toward Nearra and tugged on her arm, trying to dispel whatever enchantment held her fast. She refused to budge. Suddenly she spoke a most strange and wonderful-sounding word: Tarke-melhion. The next thing I knew, a glorious copper dragon stood before us. The copper quickly joined the battle and breathed on the ogre. Before the ogre could stop himself, he inhaled. He tried to raise his club, but he was hardly moving at all! The dragon laughed. "You may call me Raedon," he told us. "I have stopped the ogre with what in the common tongue would be called slow gas. The ogre will still move but at only a fraction of his normal speed. This will give you all ample time to get away." And so we did. I thought we would be safe with

The Copper Dragon's Lair

The entrance to a copper's lair is usually a cave, concealed by rocks and boulders. Once inside, you immediately find yourself immersed in a labyrinth of tunnels and hallways, which completely turn you about. You find yourself forever walking in circles, reaching dead ends, and retracing your steps. Brilliant fun!

Once you come upon the correct corridor, you will find yourself in a medium-sized room, which is the main foyer. This room leads into the main entertaining chamber. It is here that you might find the copper dragon, lounging back and tickling its own fancy with its wit. If the dragon needs a quick escape, it will dash through a secret door into an escape tunnel. This tunnel leads around the maze, and it is a straight route, then, to the escape exit. If you can find the outside entrance to this secret tunnel, it might be best to enter the dragon's lair here and avoid the maze.

And you'd better laugh! The copper dragon will be angry if you don't act like his stories are the most entertaining you've ever heard.

Combat

Coppers would much rather tell a joke than fight a battle. Remember, metallics, especially coppers, do not like to harm others. Coppers would much rather taunt, humiliate, and tease until their foes are simply frustrated into giving up and running away. But when threatened directly, a copper dragon will fight to the bitter end, using every trick it knows.

Typical Copper Dragon Lair

Size of lair varies with size of dragon

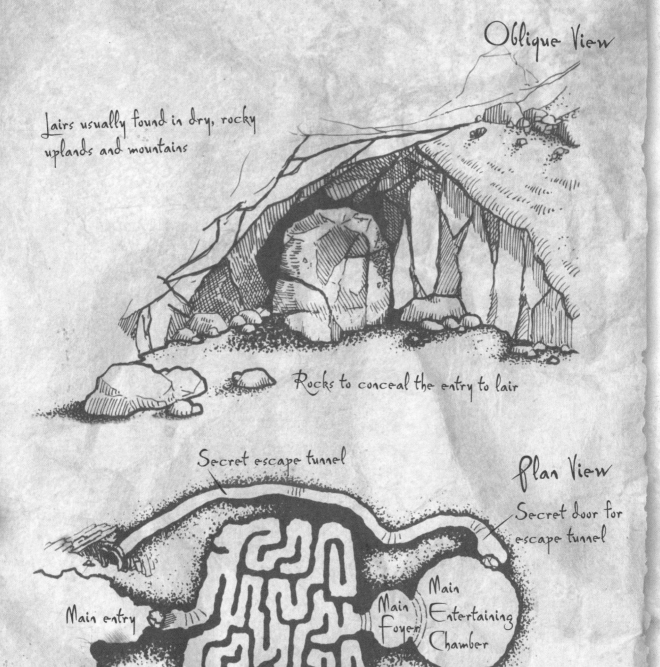

Oblique View

Lairs usually found in dry, rocky uplands and mountains

Rocks to conceal the entry to lair

Secret escape tunnel

Plan View

Secret door for escape tunnel

Main entry

Main Foyer

Main Entertaining Chamber

Prankster designed entrance for guests

THE GOLD DRAGON

Of all the metallic dragons, the gold dragon is perhaps the most dedicated to defeating evil. The gold dragon goes about its purpose in a very unassuming way. Although its true dragon form is spectacular, the gold dragon chooses to spend most of its time in human form.

The gold dragon's motivation is simple. When in this form, the dragon listen for stories of dangerous or evil creatures. Once the gold dragon has detected evil, it reveals its true form and doles out the punishment. The gold dragon may simply have the evildoer placed in a dungeon, or depending on the nature of the crime and if the scoundrel fights back, the gold dragon may even be forced to kill. The gold dragon does not relish this task, but will do so in order to defeat an evil foe.

Gold dragons do not eat any living creatures.

The cone of weakness renders those within its vapors totally harmless. This, of course, would be the gold dragon's preferred method of capturing an evildoer and transporting it to a prison or dungeon for punishment.

GOLD DRAGON FACTS

Maximum Height	22 feet
Maximum Weight	1,280,000 pounds
Maximum Wingspan	135 feet
Breath Weapon	Cone of weakness and fire
Favorite Foods	Small gems and pearls
Habitat	Anywhere! Prefer secluded lairs
Enemy	Evildoers everywhere
Favorite Treasure	Art, especially painting and sculpture

Gold dragons are graceful and wise. They smell like saffron and incense. Old dragons' eyes have the appearance of molten gold.

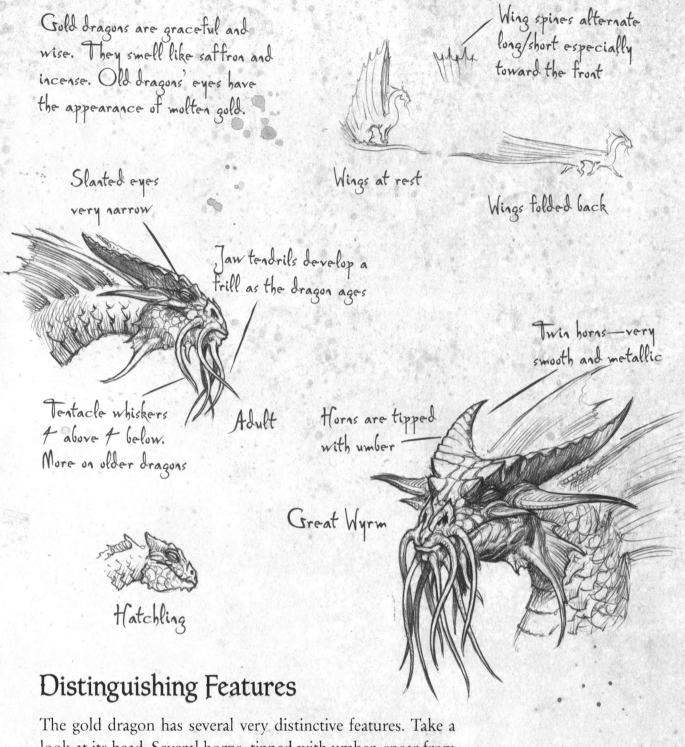

Wing spines alternate long/short especially toward the front

Wings at rest

Wings folded back

Slanted eyes very narrow

Jaw tendrils develop a frill as the dragon ages

Tentacle whiskers 4 above 4 below. More on older dragons

Adult

Twin horns—very smooth and metallic

Horns are tipped with umber

Great Wyrm

Hatchling

Distinguishing Features

The gold dragon has several very distinctive features. Take a look at its head. Several horns, tipped with umber, spear from the sides, and two prominent horns rear back along the dragon's head. Now look at its chin! Tentacle whiskers sprout from the bottom and top of the gold dragon's jaw, like a trembling beard and mustache. But the gold dragon's wings are perhaps its most fascinating feature. They are wide at the shoulders and more narrow at the tail and, when in flight, ripple as if they are swimming instead of flying through the air.

Eggs

Gold dragon eggs must be kept in an open flame.

Wyrmlings

Gold dragon wyrmlings may have two sets of parents. Their birth parents may take care of them for some number of years, taking extreme interest in their offspring's education. At some point, though, the parents may send the wyrmling to live with foster parents. This allows the parents to set off on their own quests, while exposing the wyrmling to new experiences.

Upon hatching, a gold dragon wyrmling does not yet have the horns or tentacle whiskers that so distinguish its elders.

Adults

Unlike many dragons, gold dragons have a very firm societal structure. The gold dragon hierarchy always has one gold dragon as the top dragon, so to speak. The top dragon holds this position until the dragon either passes on or steps down. At that time, another top dragon is chosen. All the gold dragons get together and decide who should be the next leader of their kind. Sometimes two dragons may be chosen, and if that is the case, the dragons will share the duties of top dragon.

The position is a noble one, and not all that strenuous. Most gold dragons behave well, so the top dragon does not need to keep order. Instead, the top dragon dispenses advice and wisdom to those gold dragons who ask for it, helping the gold dragons to make the right choices.

Gold dragons become more wise and worldly as they age. Their interests are vast, and their knowledge great. They have no problem passing on what they've learned over the centuries, and they may even take the guise of a scholarly professor in order to spread their knowledge at some bastion of higher learning for humans.

Typical Gold Dragon Lair

Size of lair varies with size of dragon

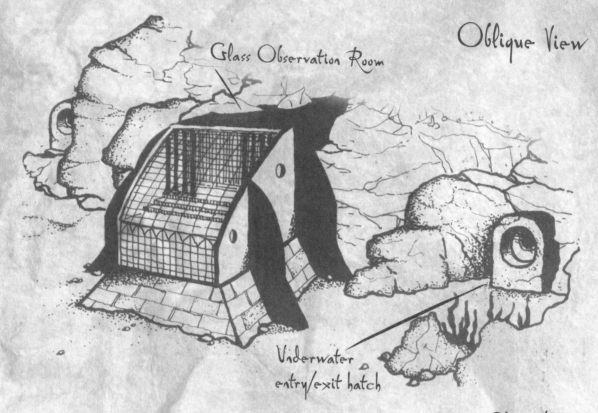

Oblique View

Glass Observation Room

Underwater entry/exit hatch

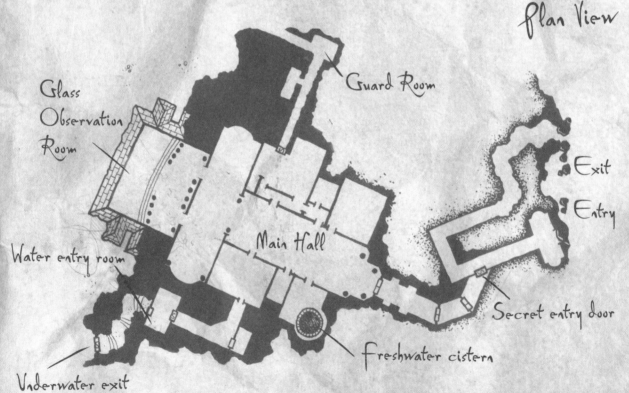

Plan View

Guard Room

Glass Observation Room

Exit

Entry

Water entry room

Main Hall

Secret entry door

Underwater exit

Freshwater cistern

The Gold Dragon's Lair

Made of stone, the gold dragon's lair is a marvel of chambers that serve a variety of functions. Unlike many dragons, who might have just a few crudely dug holes in which to live, the gold dragon's lair has a main hall, a banquet hall, a resting chamber, a study, a kitchen, a lobby, a storage room, perhaps even a room for bathing and taking care of, er, um, bodily functions. Each room is well constructed and beautifully decorated. Gold dragons love art, and the dragon displays its art very tastefully in its lair—paintings, sculptures, vases—a wonderful assortment. Gold dragons may even have a glass observatory, especially if they live underwater. From here, they can watch the world as it passes by and pick and choose how they want to get involved.

Combat

Gold dragons usually talk to their enemies before engaging them in combat. They do not like to fight unnecessarily. They will cast spells over their foes to determine whether they are lying, and if they are, then, and only then, will they attack.

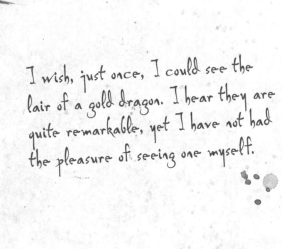

I wish, just once, I could see the lair of a gold dragon. I hear they are quite remarkable, yet I have not had the pleasure of seeing one myself.

THE SILVER DRAGON

The silver dragon is a true friend to all. In fact, the silver dragon enjoys human and elf companionship so much that it often takes the form of a human or elf and lives among them for a large portion of its life. That doesn't mean that the silver dragon thinks that nondragons are similar in intellect or strength. Just like all dragons, they believe they are the most superior creatures in the world. Unlike most dragons, however, they do recognize their limitations, such as their huge size. They do cherish one ability unique to dragons: Silvers love to fly, and they can soar for hours through the cold, wintry skies.

It will stop you in your tracks—literally! Once enfolded in its vapor, your body parts will freeze and you will be unable to move for several moments.

Because silver dragons spend very little time in their lairs, their treasures must be small enough to travel with them.

SILVER DRAGON FACTS

Maximum Height	22 feet
Maximum Weight	1,280,000 pounds
Maximum Wingspan	150 feet
Breath Weapon	Paralyzing gas; cone of cold
Favorite Foods	Just about anything; they especially like to taste new things
Habitat	High, lofty places–the cooler the better
Enemy	Red dragons
Favorite Treasure	Beautifully crafted jewelry or finely woven fabrics

Distinguishing Features

Silver dragons and white dragons look very much alike from below, and their soft, muted colors are almost indistinguishable. But you'll notice a silver's scales sparkle in the sunlight, and its wings are smooth and gently curved. The silver dragon also has two "fingers" above each wing, whereas the white dragon has only one.

The silver dragon has a magnificent frill that begins at the top of its head and flows all the way down its long, graceful neck and body to the very tip of its tail. The frill closest to the dragon's body is a lighter, silvery color, and the color becomes deeper and more purple in hue toward the edge.

Two long, smooth silver horns with black tips

Neck comb or frill is grand with black tipped spines

Ear frill has black-tipped spines

Chin frill gives look of goatee

Tongue long and pointed, not forked

Teeth don't show when the mouth is closed

Silver dragons are regal and statuesque. Old dragons have eyes that look like orbs of mercury. Silver dragons are also called shield dragons due to the plates on their heads. They smell like rain.

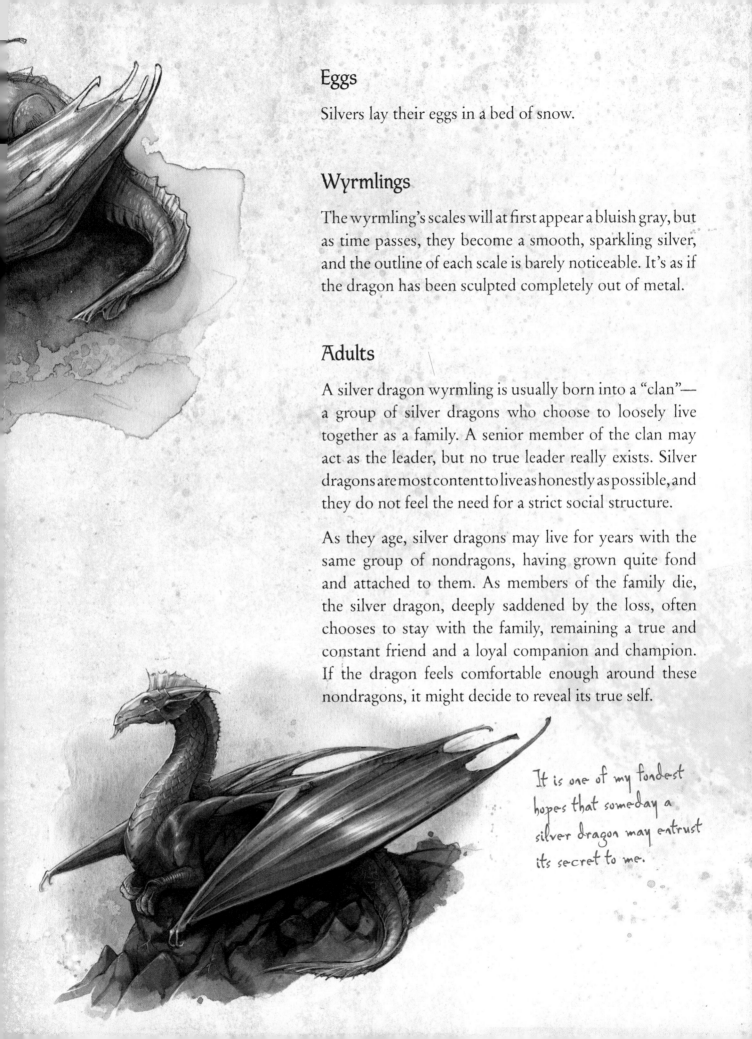

Eggs

Silvers lay their eggs in a bed of snow.

Wyrmlings

The wyrmling's scales will at first appear a bluish gray, but as time passes, they become a smooth, sparkling silver, and the outline of each scale is barely noticeable. It's as if the dragon has been sculpted completely out of metal.

Adults

A silver dragon wyrmling is usually born into a "clan"— a group of silver dragons who choose to loosely live together as a family. A senior member of the clan may act as the leader, but no true leader really exists. Silver dragons are most content to live as honestly as possible, and they do not feel the need for a strict social structure.

As they age, silver dragons may live for years with the same group of nondragons, having grown quite fond and attached to them. As members of the family die, the silver dragon, deeply saddened by the loss, often chooses to stay with the family, remaining a true and constant friend and a loyal companion and champion. If the dragon feels comfortable enough around these nondragons, it might decide to reveal its true self.

It is one of my fondest hopes that someday a silver dragon may entrust its secret to me.

The Silver Dragon's Lair

The main entrance of the silver dragon's lair can be only approached by air, which, of course, is no hardship for the silver dragon. From there, a narrow hallway bends around to the main entertaining area, a large cavernous room in which the dragon will relax with its guests. Off this entertaining area is a storage room, as well as a vault, and beyond that lies the dragon's sleeping chamber. The lair also includes a study and library, a shrine room, a smaller storage room, and two clinic rooms. Here, the dragon can offer help and protection to anyone who needs it.

No dragon's lair is ever complete without an escape route, and the silver dragon has one of those as well. A narrow tunnel leads from the back of the main living area and winds its way through the mountain in which the lair is built. The tunnel opens up to a cliff, where the dragon can then fly free.

Combat

Silver dragons do not go out of their way to bring justice to the world; rather, they wait for people to ask them for help. That does not mean that a silver dragon will not jump into the fray if it spots a bit of danger. But unlike the gold dragon, who will try to root out evil in order to banish it, the silver dragon lives peacefully with others. The silver dragon does not like to witness any injustice, and if it does, it will take action. The silver dragon is more concerned with protecting the humans it has come to care for than in spending its life looking for evil.

Typical Silver Dragon Lair
Size of lair varies with size of dragon

Oblique View

Aerial entry

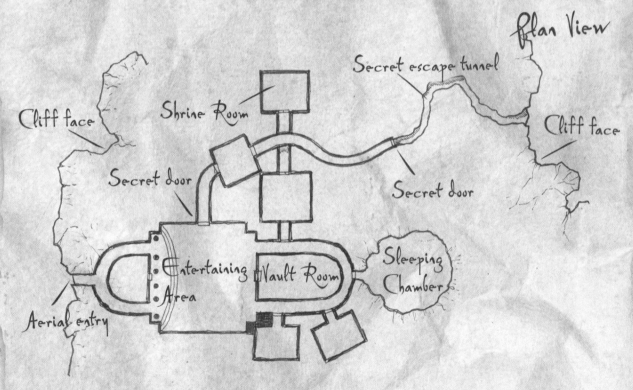

Plan View

Secret escape tunnel

Cliff face

Shrine Room

Cliff face

Secret door

Secret door

Sleeping Chamber

Entertaining Vault Room

Area

Aerial entry

Now you have met the ten true dragons—the five chromatics and the five metallics. But these are simply the basics. Dragons are supreme, mythical, magical creatures, and you can't expect them to act a certain way. In fact, when it comes to dragons, my advice would be to expect the unexpected! But keep this guide with you at all times for reference. It will give you some suggestions as to how to handle these wondrous beasts!

Sindri

P.S. I met a young bard by the name of Tim Waggoner at the Pit in Ravenscar last night. After I told Master Waggoner all about my adventures, he asked if he could scribe the tales himself to share them with the world. I'm too busy right now with my studies, and so I agreed. I told him to call it Sindri: the Greatest Kender Wizard Who Ever Lived, but he said Temple of the Dragonslayer would be a better title. If you stop by Uncle Kenneth's book shop, see if you can find a copy.

With fondest wishes to

Mother, Aunt Moonbeam, Uncle Turtledove, Cousin Phadri, Cousin Dorny, Uncle Climstrider, dearly departed Uncle Oscar, Great-Uncle Wimbog-chaser, Great-great-great-great-great-great-great-great-uncle Mildred, Uncle Oliver, Aunt Toadwyn, Uncle Barty (RIP), Great-Aunt Chauncey, Phineas, Barlow, Gisella, Nibbles, Cousin Sinclair, Grandpa Rex, Hinky, Cookie, Bitty, Lisa, Aunt Trutkoff, Grandmother Trumbauer, Grandfather Hephdeezee, and of course, Little Bob.

Text by
Lisa Trutkoff Trumbauer

Edited by
Nina Hess

Cover art by
Darrell Riche

Interior art by
Emily Fiegenschuh, Todd Lockwood, Jim Nelson,
Vinod Rams, Darrell Riche, Eva Widermann, Sam Wood

Cartography by
Todd Gamble

Art Direction by
Kate Irwin

Graphic Design by
Lisa Hanson

Don't miss these other books in the Practical Guide family!

Visit our web site at www.mirrorstonebooks.com

A Practical Guide to Dragons
©2006 Wizards.

Printed in the U.S.A.
First Printing: September 2006
Library of Congress Catalog
Card Number: 2005935984
9 8 7 6 5 4
US ISBN: 0-7869-4164-2
ISBN-13: 978-0-7869-4164-3
620-957437200-001-EN

U.S., CANADA, ASIA, PACIFIC,
& LATIN AMERICA
Wizards of the Coast, Inc.
P.O. Box 707
Renton, WA 98057-0707
+1-800-324-6496

EUROPEAN HEADQUARTERS
Hasbro UK Ltd
Caswell Way
Newport, Gwent NP9 0YH
GREAT BRITIAN
Please keep this address for your records.